Kitty Cat, Kitty Cat,
Are You Going to Sleep?

BY Bill Martin Jr and Michael Sampson

ILLUSTRATED BY Laura J. Bryant

Marshall Cavendish Children

Marshall Cavendish Corporation, 99 White Plains Road, Tarrytown, NY 10591
www.marshallcavendish.us/kids

Library of Congress Cataloging-in-Publication Data

Martin, Bill, 1916-2004.
Kitty Cat, kitty Cat, are you going to sleep? / by Bill Martin Jr and
Michael Sampson ; illustrated by Laura J. Bryant. — 1st ed.
p. cm.
Summary: A young cat is distracted by many things while getting ready for bed at night.
ISBN 978-0-7614-5946-0
[1. Stories in rhyme. 2. Bedtime—Fiction. 3. Cats—Fiction.] I. Sampson, Michael R. II. Bryant, Laura J., ill. III.
Title.
PZ8.3.M3988Kh 2011
[E]—dc22
2010025274

The text of this book is set in Classical Garamond.
The illustrations are rendered in watercolor paints and colored pencils on Strathmore paper.
Book design by Anahid Hamparian
Editor: Margery Cuyler

Printed in China [E]
First edition
1 3 5 6 4 2

To Michelle
—M.S.

To Andy and Andria
—L.J.B.

"**Kitty Cat, Kitty Cat,**
the day is almost done."

"Not yet, Mother,
I still can see the sun."

"Kitty Cat, Kitty Cat,
I am calling you."

"I know, Mother,
let's play peekaboo!"

"Kitty Cat, Kitty Cat,
are you in the tub?"

"Not yet, Mother,
I do not like to scrub."

"Kitty Cat, Kitty Cat,
did you wash your face?"

"Not yet, Mother,
I'm in outer space."

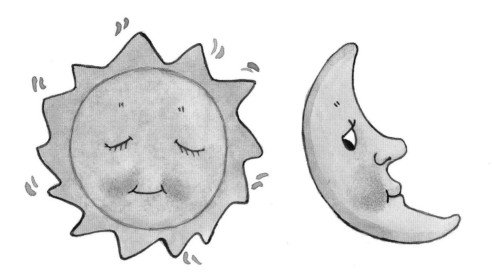

"Kitty Cat, Kitty Cat,
put on your night clothes."

"Not yet, Mother,
I'm playing with my toes."

"Kitty Cat, Kitty Cat,
have you brushed your teeth?"

"Not yet, Mother,
come look underneath!"

"Kitty Cat, Kitty Cat,
it's time to read a book."

"Okay, Mother,
I know where to look."

"Kitty Cat, Kitty cat,
lay down your sleepy head."

"Okay, Mother,
I guess it's time for bed."

"Kitty Cat, Kitty Cat,
you've finally closed your eyes."

"That's right, Mother,
time for lullabies."

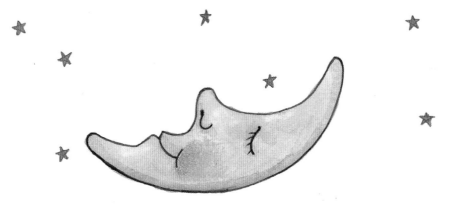

"Kitty Cat, Kitty Cat,
I'm turning out the light."

"Good night, Mother,
I will sleep *sooo* tight."